Angelina Ballerina

For Tara   KH

To my aunt, Catherine Hope Beddington, with love   HC

VIKING/PUFFIN

Published by the Penguin Group
Penguin Books Ltd, 80 Strand, London WC2R 0RL, England
Penguin Putnam Inc., 375 Hudson Street, New York, New York 10014, USA
Penguin Books Australia Ltd, 250 Camberwell Road, Camberwell, Victoria 3124, Australia
Penguin Books Canada Ltd, 10 Alcorn Avenue, Toronto, Ontario, Canada M4V 3B2
Penguin Books India (P) Ltd, 11 Community Centre, Panchsheel Park, New Delhi – 110 017, India
Penguin Books (NZ) Ltd, Cnr Rosedale and Airborne Roads, Albany, Auckland, New Zealand
Penguin Books (South Africa) (Pty) Ltd, 24 Sturdee Avenue, Rosebank 2196, South Africa

Penguin Books Ltd, Registered Offices: 80 Strand, London WC2R 0RL, England

www.penguin.com

First published by Aurum Press Ltd 1983
Published by Viking 2001
1 3 5 7 9 10 8 6 4 2
Published in Puffin Books 2001
3 5 7 9 10 8 6 4

Printed in Italy by Printer Trento Srl

British Library Cataloguing in Publication Data
A CIP catalogue record for this book is available from the British Library

ISBN 0–670–91152–6 Hardback
ISBN 0–140–56861–1 Paperback

To find out more about Angelina, visit her web site at **www.angelinaballerina.com**

Angelina Ballerina

Story by **Katharine Holabird** Illustrations by **Helen Craig**

VIKING

PUFFIN BOOKS

More than anything else in the world, Angelina loved to dance. She danced all the time and she danced everywhere, and often she was so busy dancing that she forgot about the other things she was supposed to be doing.

Angelina's mother was always calling to her, "Angelina, it's time to tidy up your room now," or "Please get ready for school now, Angelina." But Angelina never wanted to go to school. She never wanted to do anything but dance.

One night Angelina even danced in her dreams, and when she woke up in the morning, she knew that she was going to be a real ballerina some day.

When Mrs Mouseling called Angelina for breakfast,
Angelina was standing on her bed doing curtsies.

When it was time for school, Angelina was trying on her mother's hats and making sad and funny faces at herself in the mirror.
"You're going to be late again, Angelina!" cried Mrs Mouseling.

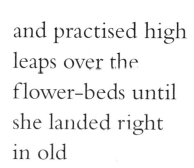

But Angelina did not care. She skipped over rocks

and practised high leaps over the flower-beds until she landed right in old

Mrs Hodgepodge's pansies and got a terrible scolding.

At playtime she twirled and spun across the playground so fast that none of the little boys in her class could catch her and they were all very cross.

After school she did a beautiful arabesque in the kitchen and knocked over a jug of milk and a plate of her mother's best Cheddar cheese pies.

"Oh Angelina, your dancing is nothing but a nuisance!" exclaimed her mother.

She sent Angelina straight upstairs to her room and went
to have a talk with Mr Mouseling. Mrs Mouseling shook
her head and said, "I just don't know what to do
about Angelina." Mr Mouseling thought awhile and
then he said, "I think I may have an idea."

That same afternoon Mr and Mrs Mouseling
went out together before the shops shut.

The next morning at breakfast Angelina
found a large box with her name on it.

Inside the box was a pink ballet dress and a pair of pink ballet slippers. Angelina's father smiled at her kindly. "I think you are ready to take ballet lessons," he said.

Angelina was so excited that she jumped straight up in the air and landed with one foot in her mother's sewing basket.

The very next day Angelina took her pink slippers and ballet dress and went to her first lesson at Miss Lilly's Ballet School. There were nine other little girls in the class and they all practised curtsies and pliés and ran around the room together just like fairies. Then they skipped and twirled about until it was time to go home.

"Congratulations, Angelina," said Miss Lilly. "You are a good little dancer and if you work hard you may grow up to be a real ballerina one day."

Angelina ran all the way home to give her mother a big hug.
"I'm the happiest little mouse in the world today!" she said.

From that day on, Angelina came downstairs when her mother called her, she tidied her room, and she went to school on time.

She helped her mother
make Cheddar cheese pies

and she even let the boys catch her
in the playground sometimes.

Angelina was so busy dancing at Miss Lilly's that she didn't need to dance at suppertime or bedtime or on the way to school any more. She went every day to her ballet lessons and worked very hard for many years …

... until at last she became the famous ballerina
Mademoiselle Angelina, and people came from
far and wide to enjoy her lovely dancing.

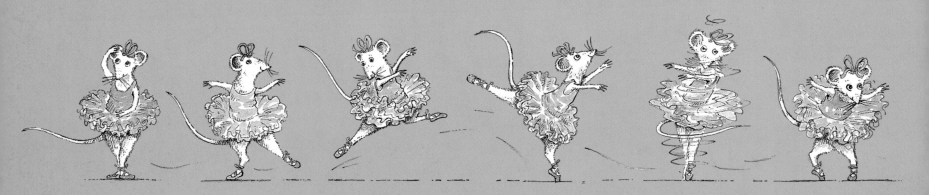